Ladybird Readers

The Cheetah's Whisker

Series Editor: Sorrel Pitts
Text adapted by Adékúnmi Qlátúnjí
Illustrated by Moka Celess
Song lyrics by Naomi Rainbow

LADYBIRD BOOKS

UK | USA | Canada | Ireland | Australia
India | New Zealand | South Africa

Ladybird Books is part of the Penguin Random House group of companies
whose addresses can be found at global.penguinrandomhouse.com.
www.penguin.co.uk   www.puffin.co.uk   www.ladybird.co.uk

Penguin
Random House
UK

Text adapted from *Tales from Africa* by Nii Ayikwei Parkes, first published by Puffin Books, 2017
This Ladybird Readers version first published by Ladybird Books Ltd, 2022
001

Original copyright © Nii Ayikwei Parkes, 2017
Text copyright © Ladybird Books Ltd, 2022
Illustrations copyright © Ladybird Books Ltd, 2022

Printed in Italy

The authorized representative in the EEA is Penguin Random House Ireland,
Morrison Chambers, 32 Nassau Street, Dublin D02 YH68

A CIP catalogue record for this book is available from the British Library

ISBN: 978–0–241–53361–1

All correspondence to:
Ladybird Books
Penguin Random House Children's
One Embassy Gardens, 8 Viaduct Gardens, London SW11 7BW

Ladybird Readers

The Cheetah's Whisker

Adapted from *Tales From Africa*
by K. P. Kojo

Picture words

Abeba

Mother

Father

Gelila

Girma

Elene

Grandma

Ethiopia

cheetah

whisker

love potion

savannah

climb

Abeba lived in a beautiful village in Ethiopia, with her mother and father.

Abeba loved her parents and she loved playing with her friends in the village. She was very happy.

One very sad day,
Abeba's mother died.

Abeba was very sad. She stopped playing with her friends and only played with her father.

After two years, Abeba's father said,
"I met a nice woman called Gelila
and I want to marry her."

"Gelila has two children," he said, "a daughter called Elene and a son called Girma. They are your new brother and sister!"

Abeba was not happy when Gelila, Girma and Elene came to live with her. She did not want a new family.

13

Abeba did not like Girma because all of her friends wanted to play with him.

She did not like Elene because she wore all her old clothes.

Gelila was very nice to Abeba, but Abeba did not want to talk to her or eat her food.

Abeba visited Grandma for
a few days.

"Grandma, I don't like my new
family," Abeba said. "Gelila doesn't
love me, but my father loves
her and her children."

"Do you want Gelila to love you?"
Grandma asked.

Abeba thought hard about this
question. Then she slowly said,
"Yes."

"Then, let's make a love potion," Grandma said.

Abeba was excited.
"What a good idea!" she said.

"A love potion is not easy to make," Grandma said. "I need a cheetah's whisker. Can you get one?"

Abeba felt very afraid but she wanted to make the love potion.

"Yes . . ." she said.

In the morning Abeba left Grandma's village to look for a cheetah. She walked and walked.

She came to some long grass. It was the savannah.

Soon, Abeba heard a river.

"Cheetahs like to drink from rivers," she thought.

She climbed up a tree to look.
Then, the grass moved . . .

It was a cheetah! It sat by the river.

Abeba watched the cheetah all day. In the evening, it went back to the river for a drink.

Abeba went back to Grandma's house. That night they made dinner.

"Does the cheetah want some food?" Abeba thought.

She put some meat in a bag.

In the morning, Abeba went back to the tree and threw the meat to the sleeping cheetah.

When the cheetah woke up,
it walked to the meat and ate it.

Then the cheetah went to the river for a drink.

Abeba went back with more meat.
She threw it to the cheetah again.
The cheetah looked happy.

One day, Abeba stayed near
the cheetah.

Every day, Abeba moved nearer
and nearer to the animal.
Now, she was not afraid. She was
the cheetah's friend.

One day, Abeba sat next to
the cheetah when it slept.
Then, she slowly took one of
its whiskers.

Abeba ran to Grandma's house. She was sad to leave her new friend, but she felt excited about making the love potion.

"Grandma! I have it! I have a cheetah's whisker!" Abeba said. "Let's make the love potion!"

Grandma laughed.

"How did you get a cheetah's whisker?" she asked.

"Every day, I was nice to the cheetah, and every day the cheetah liked me more and more," Abeba answered. "When we were friends, I took its whisker."

Grandma smiled and said,
"Abeba, you don't need a love potion.
You waited and you were nice.
Then, the cheetah came to you."

"You must wait and be nice to Gelila, Elene and Girma because it's important to your father. It's easier than making a love potion!"

Abeba went home to her
new family. She was happy
to see them.

Activities

The key below describes the skills practiced in each activity.

 Spelling and writing

Reading

Speaking

Listening*

Critical thinking

Singing*

Preparation for the Cambridge Young Learners exams

*To complete these activities, listen to the audio downloads available at **www.ladybirdeducation.co.uk**

1 Match the words to the pictures.

1 Abeba

2 Father

3 Grandma

4 Gelila

5 Elene

6 Girma

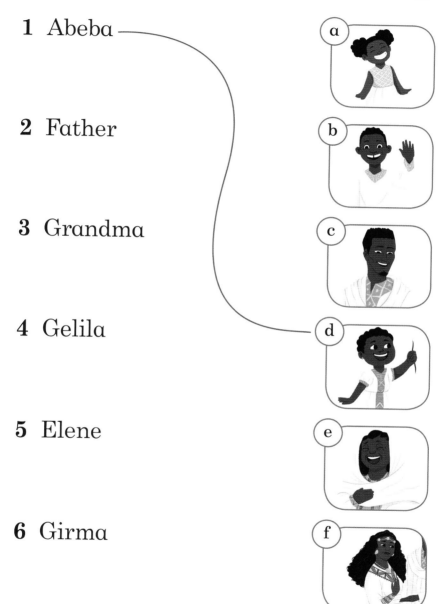

a

b

c

d

e

f

2 Circle the correct words.

1 Abeba lived in a beautiful village in **Egypt.** / **Ethiopia.**

2 She lived with her **grandma** / **mother** and her father.

3 Abeba loved her parents and she was very **happy.** / **sad.**

4 She loved playing with her **friends** / **family** in the village.

3 Talk about the two pictures with a friend. How are they different?

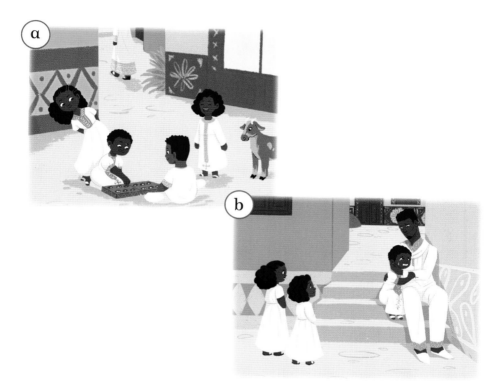

a

b

In picture a, Abeba is happy. In picture b, she is sad.

4 **Complete the sentences.**
Write a—d. 📖

1 Abeba did not want ....c........

2 Abeba didn't like
Girma because ....

3 She didn't like Elene because ....

4 Gelila was very nice to Abeba, ...

a all of her friends wanted to play
with him.

b but Abeba did not want to talk
to her.

c a new family.

d she wore all her old clothes.

5 Who said this?

Abeba   Father   Grandma

1 "I don't like my new family,"

said .... Abeba ....

2 "I want to marry Gelila,"

said ....

3 "Do you want Gelila to love you?"

asked ....

4 "I have a cheetah's whisker,"

said ....

5 "You don't need a love potion,"

said ....

51

6 Look, match, and write the words.

1. Grandma's — village

2. a love — potion

3. a good — idea

4. a cheetah's — whisker

1 _Grandma's village_

2

3

4

7 Find the words.

cheetah
whisker
village
river
savannah

kfozt**cheetah**beyvillagetrhgrwysavannaholoriverkewhisker

8 Ask and answer the questions with a friend.

1 *Where did Abeba walk?*

She walked to the savannah.

2 What did she hear?

She heard . . .

3 Why did she climb up a tree?

Because she wanted . . .

9 Write the correct form of the verbs.

"Cheetahs like to drink from rivers,"
Abeba ___thought___ **(think)**.

She _____ **(climb)** up a tree
to look. Then, the grass moved . . .
It _____ **(be)** a cheetah!
It _____ **(sit)** by the river.

Abeba _____ **(watch)**
the cheetah all day.

10 Listen, and ✓ the boxes.

1 What did Abeba do when she was sad?

a

b  ✓

c

2 Whose village did Abeba visit?

a

b

c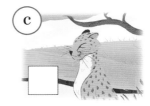

3 Where did Abeba climb?

a

b

c

4 What did Abeba see in the savanah?

a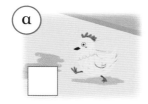

b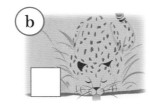

c

11 Look at the picture and read the questions. Write the answers.

1 Where is Abeba?

She is at __Grandma's house__.

2 What is Grandma making?

She is making _____.

3 What is Abeba doing?

_____ in the bag.

12 Order the story. Write 1—4. 📖

.... Abeba went back with more meat.
She threw it to the cheetah again.

.... One day, Abeba sat next to
the cheetah. Then, she slowly
took one of its whiskers.

...1... Abeba went back to the tree, and
threw the meat to the cheetah.
The cheetah walked to the meat
and ate it.

.... Every day, Abeba moved nearer
and nearer to the animal.
She was the cheetah's friend now.

13 Read the story.
Choose the right words and write
them on the lines. 📖 ✏️ ⭐

1	did	were	does
2	on	to	for
3	like	liking	liked
4	its	my	your

"How [1] ___did___ you get a

cheetah's whisker?" Grandma asked.

"Every day, I was nice [2] _____

the cheetah, and every day the cheetah

[3] _____ me more and more,"

Abeba answered. "When we were friends,

I took [4] _____ whisker."

14 Read the questions. Write answers using the words in the box.

> new family   cheetah
>
> sad   waited and was nice

1 Who was Abeba's new friend?

The cheetah was Abeba's new friend.

2 Why did the cheetah come to her?

3 How did she feel to leave her new friend?

4 Who was Abeba happy to see at the end of the story?

15 **Look at the letters. Write the words.** 📖 ✏️

(x i e c t d e)

1 Abeba was ‎ excited about making the love potion.

(s a y e)

2 "A love potion is not _____ to make," said Grandma.

(c i n e)

3 "You must wait and be _____ to Gelila."

(p y h p a)

4 Abeba was _____ to see her new family.

16 Listen, and write the answers.

1 What did Abeba see?

A cheetah

2 Where was the cheetah?

3 Where was Abeba?

4 Did the cheetah run after Abeba?

5 When did Abeba see the cheetah again?

17 Sing the song.

Abeba didn't like her new family,
Her Grandma knew.
She asked Abeba a question,
"Do you want Gelila to love you?"

"Abeba, you waited in the tree,
You watched the cheetah. It did not see!
Abeba, you were nice, too,
Then, the cheetah came to you."

Abeba went to the cheetah.
She threw it food to eat.
Every day Abeba moved nearer.
The cheetah liked the meat.

"Abeba, you waited in the tree,
You watched the cheetah. It did not see!
Abeba, you were nice, too,
Then, the cheetah came to you."

Visit www.ladybirdeducation.co.uk
for more FREE Ladybird Readers resources

✓ Digital edition of every title

✓ Audio tracks (US/UK)

✓ Answer keys

✓ Lesson plans

✓ Role-plays

✓ Classroom display material

✓ Flashcards

✓ User guides

Register and sign up to the newsletter to receive your FREE classroom resource pack!

To access the audio and digital versions of this book:

1 Go to **www.ladybirdeducation.co.uk**
2 Click "Unlock book"
3 Enter the code below

gjmVm03lx7